Modge & Podge

Helen Muir

pictures by Margarita Gluzberg

Dial Books for Young Readers · New York

Deep down, Emma Jones was a nice girl, but nothing she had seemed to please her. Every day she complained about something. And as the day of her birthday came nearer, the complaining grew worse than ever before.

"I want a puppy, Mommy. Mommy, why can't I have a puppy? Please?" Emma pleaded. "Oh, Mom . . . *please*."

Her mother thought she wasn't old enough to look after a puppy. "If you have a dog, you must take care of it," she said. "You have to remember his mealtimes, you have to take him for walks, and you have to love him very much."

"I would love him," Emma promised, "oh, I would."

But on her birthday morning
there was no puppy for Emma.
Her present was a big brown monkey.

He had long arms, a long swinging
tail, a small red tongue, and a
really naughty look. But he was stuffed.

"I don't want a toy monkey," Emma said, complaining all
the way to the stores with her mother. "I want a real one."

When they got home she
punched the monkey in the
nose and she threw him to the
back of the toy cupboard. His
ear was torn on a sharp corner
of her farmyard game.

Emma Jones didn't care.
"He can stay there," she said.
"He's sticking his tongue out
at me."

"Poor monkey," said her mother, rescuing the wounded animal from the back of the cupboard and sitting him beside Emma for her birthday party. "Now, what are you going to call him?"

Emma's mouth was stuffed. "Er . . . Podge, Splodge . . . I'll call him Modge," she replied, reaching for another piece of cake. "His name is Modge because I don't like the look of him." She screwed up her nose and stuck her tongue out with cake crumbs on it.

It was true that having a torn ear did make Modge the monkey look very angry.

And then some awful things began to happen.

When she looked down at her plate for the last mouthful of birthday cake, it was gone. Emma couldn't understand it. She stretched for more.

"No more cake," Mrs. Jones said. "You'll be sick.

Of course Emma protested. "Modge ate my birthday cake."

"Don't be silly," her mother told her. "Modge doesn't want your cake. He's a toy monkey. He's just watching."

Emma looked at him. The monkey's cheeks were puffed up and his red tongue was sticking out.

She knew he was up to something.

At bedtime her milk spilled all over the carpet.
At lunch the next day something kept tickling everyone's
legs under the table.

"It isn't me," Emma said.

And it wasn't Emma who squirted tomato ketchup all over her father's best shirt, but it was Emma who got punished.

She was getting the blame for everything.

Who buried her shoes in the sandbox?

Who put a
strawberry jam hat
on the picture
of her grandmother?

Who wrote POOR OLD MODGE on the mirror
in her mother's beautiful new pink lipstick?

Mrs. Jones was very annoyed. "You are getting a
bit too naughty," she told Emma.

"It's Modge," Emma said. "He's a bit naughty. And I
don't like him anyway."

When they were driving home in the car, she threw the
monkey out of the window.

"That's the end of him," she said to herself.

But it wasn't.

Emma missed him.
She couldn't put Modge out of her mind.
She kept looking around for him, and of
course he wasn't there. In her dreams she
heard the little cries of the sad monkey.

Emma tried to get on without him.
She started to draw a picture of something
but it turned out to be of Modge.
She started to write a little story but it
was really only about Modge.
She wished she hadn't punched him and hurt his ear.

"What should I do now?" Emma asked her mother.

"Well," Mrs. Jones said, "you could help me set the table."

Emma put the knives and forks out. "I've done it," she told her mother. "What should I do now?"

"Where's poor old Modge?" her mother asked.

There was no reply.

Emma set out to find him.

Emma went everywhere. She searched behind garden walls and in the gutters.

She asked the postman and the window cleaner. Nobody had seen a big brown monkey with a torn ear and a red tongue sticking out.

She walked on and on.

It was raining dismally when
at last she spotted a big brown
bundle beside a garbage can.
    Curled against it for warmth
was a small brown dog. A real one.

Very gently Emma lifted
a dirty, damp Modge into
her arms.

But that lonely little stray
puppy wasn't going to lose
his only friend in the world.

He held onto one bit of Modge
and Emma held onto another bit
and they all went in together.

"If the puppy hasn't got a home," her mother said at last, "you could take care of him."

"I'll call him Podge," Emma replied. "Modge and Podge – my two favorite friends."

For Fiona and all the MacDonalds'
HM

First published in the United States 1989
by Dial Books for Young Readers
A Division of NAL Penguin Inc.
2 Park Avenue
New York, New York 10016
Published in Great Britain
by Methuen Children's Books Ltd
Text copyright © 1989 by Helen Muir
Illustrations copyright © 1989 by Margarita Gluzberg
All rights reserved
Printed in Great Britain
First Edition
(c)
1   3   5   7   9   10   8   6   4   2

Library of Congress Cataloging in Publication Data
Muir, Helen.
Modge and Podge/by Helen Muir;
illustrations by Margarita Gluzberg.
p.   cm.
Summary: Emma receives a stuffed monkey for her birthday
instead of the puppy she wanted, and doesn't realize
how much she loves it until she throws it away.
ISBN 0-8037-0584-0
[1. Toys—Fiction.   2. Monkeys—Fiction.]
I. Gluzberg, Margarita, ill. II. Title.
PZ7.M8835Mo   1989   [E]—dc19   88-7114   CIP   AC